BATTERSEA DOGS & CATS HOME

DAISY'S
story

by
Jane Clarke

RED FOX

BATTERSEA DOGS & CATS HOME: DAISY'S STORY
A RED FOX BOOK 978 1 849 41179 0

First published in Great Britain by Red Fox,
an imprint of Random House Children's Publishers UK
A Random House Group Company

This edition published 2010

5 7 9 10 8 6 4

Set in 13/20 Stone Informal

Red Fox Books are published by Random House Children's Publishers UK
61–63 Uxbridge Road, London W5 5SA

www.**randomhousechildrens**.co.uk
www.randomhouse.co.uk

Addresses for companies within The Random House Group Limited
can be found at: www.randomhouse.co.uk/offices.htm

THE RANDOM HOUSE GROUP Limited Reg. No. 954009

A CIP catalogue record for this book is available from the British Library.

The Random House Group Limited supports The Forest Stewardship
Council® (FSC®), the leading international forest-certification organisation.
Our books carrying the FSC label are printed on FSC®-certified paper.
FSC is the only forest-certification scheme supported by the leading
environmental organisations, including Greenpeace. Our
paper procurement policy can be found at
www.randomhouse.co.uk/environment

Printed   plc

Turn to page 93 for lots
of information on the
Battersea Dogs & Cats Home,
plus some cool activities!

Meet the stars of the Battersea Dogs and Cats home series to date . . .

Bailey

Misty

Chester

Rusty

Max

Daisy

A New Friend

"We're getting another dog!" Sophie
Campbell excitedly told her best friend
Eva. "I can't wait!" Sophie's ponytail
bounced as she plopped herself down on
the mat next to Morris, her Labrador.
Morris was snoozing quietly in his
favourite place in front of the living-room
fireplace. He opened one eye as Eva sat
down too, and his tail began to twitch as

the girls tickled him behind his velvety black ears.

"Does Morris know he's getting a playmate?" Eva asked.

Morris's hairy tail thumped slowly on the floor when he heard his name.

"He will soon," Sophie said, with a huge smile on her face. "Dad's on his way back from Battersea Dogs & Cats Home right now!"

"I heard an advert on the radio saying that Battersea is a rescue home full of dogs and cats. And every one of them

needs a new family to look after them
and love them!" Eva said.

"They do!" Sophie
stopped tickling
Morris, and sat
back on her
knees. Morris
grunted and
rolled onto his
back. The
underside of
his muzzle was
very grey, and
there were tufts of
white hair on his
tummy. He began to
paddle his front paws in the air.

"He paws at the air like that when he
wants to have his tummy rubbed," Sophie
told Eva. Morris's eyes closed in bliss.

"Morris listened to the Battersea Dogs & Cats Home advert with me and Mum and Dad . . ." Sophie's face went dreamy as she remembered how she'd turned to her parents with big puppy-dog eyes. "I said, 'We have to help!'" she went on. "Of course, Mum immediately said, 'No! We can't have another dog. Morris already eats us out of house and home!'" Sophie pulled a face. "That's not fair . . ."

"You told me Morris ate a whole loaf of bread once." Eva giggled as the sound of gentle doggy snores rumbled around the room. Morris had fallen fast asleep again.

"That was when he was younger," Sophie told her. "He put his front paws up on the kitchen table when he thought we couldn't see. He can't manage to do that these days, though. His legs are too stiff."

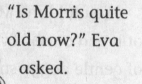

"Is Morris quite old now?" Eva asked.

"Over ten," Sophie said. "He lived here before I was born! Mum and Dad don't know his exact birthday, so he has his birthday party on the same day as me. Mum makes him his own little cake with a candle on it, but we try not to let him eat the candle . . ."

"They say a dog year is like seven human years," Eva said slowly,

"so Morris is more than seventy years old!"

"Dad said it'd be good to have another dog to be company for him in his old age." Sophie grinned. "Mum asked if that was Dad's old age or Morris's!"

"Your mum is funny," Eva laughed.

"I could tell that Mum was coming round to the idea of having another dog," Sophie said. "And you know what? We went to Battersea Dogs & Cats Home the very next day!"

"That was quick!" Eva said.

"It was Dad's day off," Sophie explained. "Of course, Mum said it was just to find out a bit more and I shouldn't get my hopes up. We took Morris too – because Dad checked on the website and it said it was really important to bring your pet to make sure it would get on with another dog."

"That's very sensible." Eva nodded.

"So we went to the Home, and a really nice man showed us round and asked us all about our house and garden, and he said he'd got a lovely little dog he thought would suit us."

Sophie smiled dreamily as she remembered. "A lovely little dog called Daisy . . ."

Not One Dog, But TWO!

"Daisy's owner got her when she was a tiny puppy," the man from the Home told the Campbell family as he led the way to the kennels. "But unfortunately the lady was allergic to dog hair! She got really bad asthma, and couldn't breathe properly when Daisy was in the same room, so she just couldn't keep Daisy, even though she loved her."

"That's
terrible!"
Sophie
sighed,
looking up at
the man as
he stopped
outside a
kennel. If I
had to give
Morris away, it

would break my heart! she thought.

"Poor Daisy doesn't like being at the
Home much," the man said. "It's much
too noisy and hectic for her. She needs a
quiet life, with an older, calmer dog she
can look up to and feel safe with."

"She'd feel safe with my dog, Morris!"
Sophie told him. "He's really old and
calm!"

She felt a tap on her shoulder and whirled round. Dad was pointing at Mum. She was crouching down, staring between the bars at a gorgeous little dog that looked a bit like a Border collie.

Daisy was sitting staring solemnly back at her, whiskers quivering. She was black all over, but for her muzzle, a heart-shaped patch on her chest and two front paws which were white.

Sophie's heart felt as if it would burst. Daisy is the cutest dog ever! she thought. But will Mum like her? She crossed her fingers behind her back.

"Awwwww!" Mum murmured. Daisy's tail twitched. There was a white tip on the end of that too! Sophie could see that Mum and Daisy's eyes were sparkling.

Dad winked at Sophie.

"What a lovely little dog!" he said to Mum. "It's a shame we're only looking today, isn't it? Daisy's so cute, she might not be here next time. Come on, Sophie, time to go home . . ."

Sophie's mum whirled round.

"Stop!" she blurted out. "Daisy can't go and live with someone else! She has to come and live with me! I mean *us*!"

Sophie and Dad looked at each other
and burst out laughing. Sophie uncrossed
her fingers.

Yip! Daisy barked a tiny bark and tried
to jump into Mum's arms. *Yip! Yip!*

The man smiled. "Our dogs are so
wonderful, people can't resist them when
they see them," he said.

"Morris will love Daisy too!" Sophie
said excitedly.

"We need to check to make sure Daisy
will be OK with Morris," the man told
them. "They can meet in the exercise
area."

"I'll get Morris out of the car," Dad said, hurrying off.

Sophie's heart was thumping. She could hardly bear to watch. She held her breath as Morris and Daisy were let off their leads. Daisy plonked herself down on her bottom and stayed frozen to the spot. Morris slowly plodded over and snuffled at Daisy, then he calmly turned away and lifted his leg against the wall of the exercise yard. He wagged his tail as he walked back to Sophie.

Daisy shot a glance at Morris, then stood up and tiptoed over to sniff at the damp patch Morris had made on the wall. She squatted down beside it, making a little puddle on the ground. When she stood up, her tail was wagging too.

"It'd be strange if people greeted each other like that," Mum laughed, making Sophie giggle.

Morris flopped down at Sophie's feet with a sigh as Daisy trotted back to the man from the Home.

"Why are they ignoring each other?" Sophie asked worriedly.

"Don't worry, that's normal," the man said. "Dogs need time to get to know each other. The important thing is that their tails are wagging, and there's no growling or biting. I think they could become very good friends!"

"So, what's the next step, if Daisy is to come and live with us?" asked Mum.

"We'll send someone to visit your home to check that it's suitable," the man told them. "I'm sure it will be . . ."

And it had been. Sophie smiled to herself.

Suddenly the front door slammed. Sophie jumped.

"Wake up, Sophie! You're in a daydream." Eva's voice was in Sophie's ear. "Your dad is back!"

On the living-room carpet, Morris stopped snoring. He opened his eyes and pricked up his ears.

"Morris! It's Daisy!" Sophie squealed. She leaped to her feet, fizzing with excitement. "Your new doggy friend has come home!"

"You are sooo lucky," Eva sighed. "My parents will only let me have one goldfish. But now you, Sophie Campbell, have not just one dog, but TWO!"

Introducing Daisy

"We're home!" Dad called. He pushed open the door to the living room. Mum raced in from the kitchen. Daisy was in Dad's arms. The little bundle of black and white fur was shaking from nose to tail.

"Awwww!" Mum, Sophie and Eva cried together.

Morris got slowly to his feet.

Woof! he barked, wagging his tail

furiously. Daisy tried to hide her head under Dad's arm.

"Shhh, Morris!" Sophie patted him on the head. "You're scaring Daisy!"

"Hello, Daisy," Mum said softly as she slowly approached the little collie. "Welcome home. This is Sophie, and Morris. You've met them before. And this is Eva . . . Say hello to Daisy, Eva."

Eva gently stroked Daisy behind the ears.

"You are so cute," she murmured.

Daisy's rubbery black nose poked over Dad's arm.

Dad gently lowered Daisy onto the carpet. Daisy took one look at Morris and shot behind Dad.

Morris put his head on one side. *Woof?* he barked softly.

Daisy peeped out from behind Dad's legs.

Sophie held her breath as Morris padded up to Daisy. He looked enormous next to her! Daisy put her tail between her legs and trembled as Morris sniffed her from top to bottom.

"I think Morris remembers meeting her," Sophie whispered to Eva as Morris wagged his tail. He lumbered off to his basket behind the settee and came back with his blue rubber ball. He dropped it at Daisy's feet.

Daisy sniffed at the gummy, slobbery ball.

Woof! Morris barked, bowing down and wagging his tail.

"He wants Daisy to play with him!" Sophie smiled. But Daisy didn't budge.

"She doesn't know how to play," Eva murmured.

Morris picked up his ball and trotted back to his basket. He settled down with a huge sigh and closed his eyes.

"We'll teach Daisy how to play with you," Sophie promised Morris. "But now it's time for a tour of the house." She scooped up Daisy. She could feel the little dog trembling in her arms.

"*Rock-a-bye Daisy,*" she crooned, stroking the ears that were so much smaller than Morris's. The little dog stopped shaking and began to relax.

"This is the living room," Sophie told her. "Dogs aren't allowed on the settee, not even when we're watching TV. I know it's unfair" – Sophie shot her dad one of her looks – "but that's the rule. You and Morris have to sit on the mat. Morris's bed is behind the settee, but he's used to sleeping in here on his own, so we thought it would be better to put your bed in here . . ."

Sophie carried
Daisy into the
kitchen.

"This is your
bed," she said
pointing to a
brand-new
fleece-lined basket
in the corner. Inside
it was a rubbery fake bone and a special
doggy toy the size and shape of a mouse.

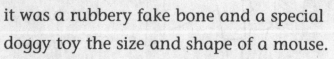

"That's such a nice surprise!" Eva
exclaimed.

"I hope you like it, Daisy!" Sophie set
the little dog down in her new basket. She
held her breath as Daisy sniffed about,
then picked up the chewy bone.

The little dog wagged her tail. Then
she spotted the mouse toy, and spat out
the chewy bone.

"It's got a squeaker in it," Sophie whispered to Eva.

Yip! Daisy barked, pouncing on the fake mouse.

The toy went *Eeeeeeek!*

Daisy dropped it and jumped into the air in surprise. She turned her head to one side, looking at the mouse quizzically. Then she pounced on it again.

Eeeeeek! it squeaked.

Daisy's tail wagged wildly.

"She loves it!" Sophie told Eva delightedly as they watched Daisy squeak the mouse again, and again, and again.

At last the little dog curled up in her basket, her head on her mouse toy.

"She's tired out," Sophie murmured, stroking Daisy's head.

"I think Daisy is happy to have a new home," Eva whispered as tiny snuffly snores echoed around the kitchen.

Sophie felt as if she might burst with happiness. When Daisy makes friends with Morris, she thought, life will be perfect!

Sweet Dreams

"I wish Daisy would wake up!" Sophie
said, wriggling impatiently. She was
sitting on the mat with her arm round
Morris, watching TV. Daisy had been
snoozing all evening. The little collie
hadn't even noticed when Eva went
home, and she'd almost fallen asleep in
her chunky chicken dinner. Morris had
gobbled up her leftovers.

"It was a big day for Daisy," Dad said. "She's worn out by all the excitement and attention."

"Oh look!" Mum exclaimed, pointing at the TV. "It's a programme about Battersea Dogs & Cats Home."

"Hey! That's the man who showed us round!" Sophie shrieked. "We met someone who is on TV. Cool!"

Morris's ears pricked up at the sounds of the dogs woofing in their kennels.

Yip! There was a little bark from the doorway. Daisy trotted into the living room and sat down on the mat next to Morris. The two dogs' heads turned to one side.

"They're watching the programme," Sophie laughed.

"Listening to it, more like," Dad said. "Dogs don't see the screen well. But perhaps they recognize some of the barks and think TV dogs are cool too!"

The advert was coming to an end.
"Can you give a dog a new home?" the
man from the Home asked.

"We can!" Sophie and her mum and
dad said together. They looked at each
other and laughed.

Woof! Morris barked.

Yip! Daisy yapped. She looked up at
Morris, then rolled over onto her back.

"She's showing Morris that she knows
he's the boss," Dad whispered.

Morris looked at
Daisy and yawned.
The he slowly
hoisted himself to
his feet, wagged his
tail and plodded
towards the back
door. Daisy sat up
and yawned too.

"Morris knows when it's his bedtime,"
Mum chuckled. She looked at Sophie.
"School tomorrow, Sophie. It's time you
went to bed too."

"But Daisy's
only just woken
up!" Sophie
protested. "I
want to teach
her how to
play!"

"There will be plenty of time for that after school tomorrow," Dad said. "Daisy is very tired today. Let her out into the garden with Morris so they can do their business, then all three of you can go to bed."

Sophie opened the back door. Morris trotted out, followed by Daisy, and made a beeline for the tree in the centre of the grass. Within a minute, both dogs were back inside. Morris headed for his basket behind the settee in the living room. Sophie could hear his contented sigh as he flopped down in it.

"Bedtime, Daisy." Sophie picked up the little collie and took her into the kitchen. She put her down next to the new basket. Daisy leaped into it, and nudged her mouse toy with her nose. Then she curled up and instantly fell fast asleep. Sophie watched as Daisy's nose began to whiffle and her paws started to twitch. Her tail wagged once in her sleep.

Sophie smiled. "Daisy's already dreaming," she said, kissing her mum and dad goodnight.

"Night-night, Sophie." Mum smiled.
"You have sweet dreams too."

It was hard for Sophie to drop off to
sleep when there was a new member of
the Campbell family in the house. What
if Daisy wakes up in the night? She might
feel lonely in the kitchen on her own! She
thought. I'd better check to see if she's
OK! She clambered out of bed and crept
downstairs and quietly pushed open the
kitchen door.

There was Mum,
sitting on
the floor
by Daisy's
basket,
gently stroking
her behind
the ears.

Mum looked up guiltily. "I was just making sure Daisy wasn't lonely," she told Sophie. "But she looks very comfortable in her little basket. It's lovely to have a new member of the family, isn't it?"

"It is," Sophie agreed, smiling down at the sleeping dog. Then she gave her mum a big hug and went back to bed and slept soundly till morning.

Sophie's bedside alarm woke her up. Her first thought was: I must check on Daisy!

Sophie's ponytail swung wildly as she leaped out of bed and dashed downstairs. The kitchen door was open a crack. She pushed it open. Her tummy did a somersault. Daisy's basket was empty!

Morris Gets Grumpy

Sophie looked around wildly. A wave of panic washed over her. Where was Daisy?

Mum's head popped round the door. She put her finger to her lips, and beckoned Sophie into the living room.

Daisy was snuggled up next to Morris in his basket! They were both fast asleep.

"Awwww!" Sophie exclaimed, going over to give them a pat.

Daisy licked at Sophie's fingers as Morris slowly opened his eyes. He tried to do his morning stretch, but Daisy was in the way. He shoved the little dog with his nose and pushed her out of his basket.

"He's not used to sharing his sleeping space," Mum commented as Morris stretched out luxuriously and went back to sleep.

Daisy looked up at Sophie and whimpered.

Sophie scooped her up for a cuddle. "Don't take any notice of Morris," she murmured. "He never likes getting up in the morning!"

Dad appeared at the door. "Nor do I." He grimaced. "If you hurry up, Sophie, I'll drop you off at school on my way to work."

"But I want to walk to school with Mum and Daisy and Morris," Sophie said, thinking how surprised her friends would be to see her with two dogs.

"Then I'd have to walk Morris and Daisy back on my own, and I've never walked two dogs together before," Mum said. "I need to practise."

Sophie's face fell.

"I'll practise today, and if it goes well, I'll bring them both with me when I pick you up this afternoon," Mum promised.

School seemed to take for ever that day. As soon as she heard the home-time buzzer, Sophie dashed to the school gates. Yaaay! Mum was standing there with Daisy and Morris! Sophie felt so proud she thought she would burst as her friends gathered round.

Everyone spoke softly so as not to upset Daisy, just like Sophie had told them to do. Daisy's little tail wagged and wagged.

"Daisy is much braver today," Eva whispered as they softly patted the little dog's head.

"That's thanks to Morris," Mum explained. "Daisy's really taken to him. She's been following him around like a shadow. Every time he went to his basket, Daisy got in too. Morris hasn't had a nap all day!"

Morris nudged at Sophie's hand and looked up at her pleadingly. His ears and tail were drooping.

"I haven't forgotten you, Morris!" Sophie giggled, giving his ears a rub. Morris's tail wagged once, slowly.

"You are so lucky to have two dogs!" Eva said again, and everyone, including Sophie, agreed.

Mum handed Daisy's lead to Sophie.

"Time to go!" she said, setting off with Morris.

Daisy tugged on the lead as Sophie said goodbye to her friends.

"It's OK, Daisy, we'll catch them up," Sophie told her.

Daisy pulled as hard as she could until they caught up with Morris, then she trotted along beside him. She kept so close that it looked as if she was glued to Morris's side. Every time Morris stopped to sniff or to water a lamppost, Daisy stopped to sniff, and make her mark too.

They were nearly home when the next-door neighbours' big tabby cat crossed the road in front of them.

"Uh-oh," Mum said. Sophie saw her
tighten her grip on Morris's lead.

Woof! Morris barked, lunging towards
the tabby.

"Watch out for Daisy!" Sophie yelled.
She pulled the little dog out of the way as
Morris tried to jump
over her to get to
the cat. Their
leads got all
tangled up
and in the
muddle, and
the cat
stalked off.

Morris sat
looking grumpy as Sophie unclipped both
dogs' leads so she could untangle them.
Then the big old Labrador got to his feet
and stomped off towards the house.

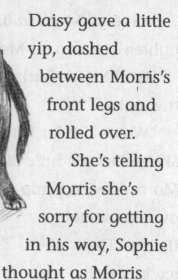

Daisy gave a little yip, dashed between Morris's front legs and rolled over.

She's telling Morris she's sorry for getting in his way, Sophie thought as Morris stumbled over Daisy.

Woof! Morris barked crossly down at her.

Daisy leaped to her feet, and accidentally tripped up Morris again! Morris's lip curled.

Grrrrr! he growled, and he gave Daisy a quick nip on her furry bottom.

Aooooo! Daisy howled, running to hide behind Sophie's legs.

Morris glared at her.

Sophie's heart sank.

"If Morris and Daisy are enemies, we'll have to take Daisy back to the Home!" she wailed.

Running Wild

"It's just a squabble," Mum reassured
Sophie.

Sophie picked up Daisy. She was
trembling from nose to tail. "Morris, you
scared Daisy," Sophie hissed.

Morris's ears and tail drooped.

"Daisy has to learn to give Morris a bit
more space, and some time on his own,
then they'll be fine together," Mum said.

"I think a walk in the woods will help."

"That will cheer them up!" Sophie agreed enthusiastically. Morris adored the woods that backed onto their garden. He knew every tree and all the fox trails, rabbit holes and badger paths. He could show Daisy around a bit.

"The weather's so lovely, I packed some cake and drinks for a little picnic," Mum said, picking up a basket she'd left in the back porch.

"Come on, Morris, there are sniffs to be sniffed!" Sophie led the way through the back garden and out of the gate into the woods.

Daisy stopped trembling and began to wag her tail as Morris bounded ahead. They followed the main path until they came to their favourite clearing in the woods at the foot of an enormous old oak tree. The sun shone through the leafy branches, dappling the earth beneath.

Mum spread out the picnic blanket on
the warm ground. Sophie put Daisy down
on the opposite side of the blanket to
Morris. Great strings of doggy slobber
dripped from Morris's jaws as he watched
Mum take out a bottle of squash and a
foil-wrapped package from the picnic
basket. Daisy's nose started to
twitch as Sophie
unwrapped the foil.

"It's chocolate cake. Chocolate is poison for dogs!" she told Daisy, sinking her teeth into the yummy cake.

Daisy sighed an enormous sigh and lay down. She stared unblinkingly at Mum and Sophie.

"She's making me feel really guilty," Sophie said. "She doesn't understand why she can't have chocolate. And nor does Morris!"

"Look in the basket," Mum told her.

Sophie peered in. There was a box of

dog biscuits at the bottom.

Morris's eyes brightened as Sophie took out the box and put a biscuit down in front of Daisy. Daisy looked at it in disgust. Sophie handed a biscuit to Morris. He gobbled it down, and another and another.

"That's all, Morris." Sophie showed him her empty open hand. Morris looked hopefully at Daisy's biscuit. The little dog began to munch daintily on it.

Suddenly there was a rustling in the branches of the oak tree. Morris pricked up his ears. A squirrel bounded along the branch and leaped across to the next tree.

Woof! Morris barked, and raced after the squirrel as fast as his old legs would carry him.

"He's hoping it will fall out of the tree!" Sophie laughed.

"He'll never catch a squirrel," Mum said with a smile. "Or anything else for that matter. He's just too slow these days, and his eyesight isn't as good as it was."

For a moment, Daisy sat staring at the place where Morris had vanished into the

woods. Then she jumped to her feet,
spitting out the remains of her biscuit,
and with a happy *yip! yip! yip!* she tore off
after Morris.

"Daisy, come back!" Sophie yelled.
Both dogs had disappeared into a tangle
of blackberry briars and stinging nettles
between the trees.

"Daisy will get lost! She doesn't know the woods," Sophie said in alarm. "I have to find her!"

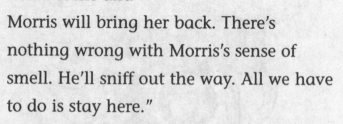

"Daisy will be fine," Mum said reassuringly. "She'll catch up with Morris and Morris will bring her back. There's nothing wrong with Morris's sense of smell. He'll sniff out the way. All we have to do is stay here."

"Morris always comes back," Sophie agreed. "Perhaps he'll be happy that Daisy has gone to help him catch squirrels," she added hopefully.

They finished
the cake and
packed
everything
away, then
Mum rolled up
the blanket
and put it in
the basket.

Sophie looked at
her watch.

"They've been
gone a long time," she said nervously. "I
hope Daisy's all right . . ."

Mum put her head on one side. "I
think I can hear them coming back," she
said. "Listen!"

Sophie held her breath. There was a
rustling in the undergrowth and Daisy
burst into the clearing.

Yip! she barked. *Yip! Yip!*

Sophie breathed a sigh of relief as she
bent down to greet the little dog. She
looked round.

"Where's Morris?" she asked, puzzled.
"Didn't you come
back with him?"

Yip! Yip!
Yip! Daisy
gripped the
arm of
Sophie's
jumper, and
tugged at it
with all her might.

Sophie felt a shiver
run down her spine. "Daisy wants me to
follow her!" she cried. "Something's
happened to Morris! Come on!"

Daisy to
the Rescue

Daisy scurried off into the woods. She
turned her head and barked over her
shoulder.

"We're right behind you!" Sophie
grabbed a dead stick and beat down a
clump of vicious-looking stinging nettles.

Yip! Daisy yapped once.

"She's telling us to hurry up!" Sophie
told Mum as Mum picked up the picnic

basket. She hooked a long spiky blackberry bramble with her stick and pushed it out of the way so that they could pass.

"Daisy's probably just found a squirrel, and wants us to know about it," Mum grumbled as the little dog led them into a thicket of hazel trees.

They were in a part of the wood Sophie didn't know. The trees grew close together and their leaves blocked out the sun.

It felt several degrees cooler than outside
in the sunshine. Spooky shadows loomed
all around them. Sophie shivered in the
gloom and looked about nervously for
Daisy. There was no sign of her. High
above them, something screeched.

Sophie and her mum jumped into
each other's arms.

"It was only a bird," Mum whispered,
untangling herself from Sophie.

A little black-and-white shadow raced up to them and danced around their feet.

Yip, yip, yip! Daisy dashed towards an old gnarled tree trunk on the other side of the thicket. She stood there with her head on one side. *Wheeep!* she whimpered, *Wheep, wheep!*

"What is it, Daisy?" Sophie asked, rushing over to her.

There in the shadows, partly hidden by a heavy branch, lay Morris. He wasn't moving.

Tears sprang to Sophie's eyes. "He's hurt!" she yelled, rushing over to him.

The old dog looked up at her and
feebly wagged his tail. Sophie could see
that one of his front paws was trapped
under the branch.

Oooop! Morris whimpered pathetically.
He was shivering from nose to tail.
Wheeep! Daisy whimpered in sympathy.

"He must have run into it, not
watching where he was going," Mum
groaned.

"He was probably looking up at a squirrel!" Sophie stroked Morris's head and murmured to him as Mum carefully felt Morris all over. He whimpered when she touched his front right leg.

"I don't think it's broken," Mum said. "He's shivering because of the shock. We need to keep him warm."

"The picnic blanket!" Sophie dived in the basket and unfolded the blanket. She draped it around Morris.

Mum took out her mobile phone and called Dad to tell him what had happened.

"Dad's coming home," she said. "Let's see if we can free Morris's paw and get him back to the house."

Sophie and Mum heaved at the branch.

"It's no good, it's too heavy!" Sophie gasped despairingly.

Daisy carefully began to scrabble at the soft ground by Morris's injured paw.

"Clever girl, Daisy," Sophie breathed. "That's the way to do it! It's OK, Morris, we can get you out of here!"

Sophie, Mum
and Daisy
carefully
scooped
the earth
away until
they could gently
ease out Morris's
trapped paw.

Daisy wagged her tail as
Morris struggled to his feet, still draped in
the blanket. *Ooooop!* he moaned, holding
up his hurt paw. It was caked with a
mixture of dirt and blood.

"That paw needs checking at the
vet's," Mum said.

Morris tried to put his weight on his
paw, but collapsed onto the ground.

"He can't walk!" Sophie groaned.

"I'll have to carry him," Mum said.

"You take Daisy, so she doesn't get lost again."

Sophie popped Daisy into the picnic basket. The little dog put her paws up on the edge of the basket and watched anxiously as Mum picked Morris up around his chest and his bottom. Morris's nose and tail stuck out from under the blanket. His tail wagged feebly as Mum staggered off under the heavy load.

"Morris weighs a ton!" Mum panted.

Dad was back from work by the time they got home.

"Morris has to go to the vet's!" Sophie told him as he took Morris from Mum.

"The car's right here," Dad said. He carefully settled Morris and the blanket onto the back seat. Morris lay there with his ears drooping. He looked very sorry for himself.

Mum jumped into the driver's seat. "We'll be at the vet's in no time at all," she told them. "Try not to worry!"

Daisy howled as the car sped away, and Sophie felt like howling too.

Best of Friends

"So, Daisy led you to Morris," Dad said, letting them into the house, "and showed you how to dig him out. That was very clever of her."

"Ever so clever. Morris was in a really overgrown part of the woods." Sophie took Daisy out of the picnic basket and gave her a big cuddle. "If it wasn't for Daisy, Morris could have been lying out

there all night before we
found him. He
might have
been dead
in the
morning."
She
shuddered.

"Morris
didn't look that
badly hurt." Dad smiled.

"And he'd stopped shaking, so the
shock was wearing off," Sophie said. "Oh!
I wish he was back home right now!" she
sighed.

"It's the rush hour," Dad reminded her.
"It will take a while for Mum to get to the
vet's. Then they'll have to wait their turn.
There's no point in worrying. We should
try to take our minds off it."

"Let's teach Daisy to play!" Sophie said.

She grabbed Daisy's squeaky mouse toy and headed for the garden.

"Fetch!" she said, throwing the toy.

Daisy scampered across the garden and grabbed the mouse.

Eeek! it squeaked.

"Good girl, Daisy! Bring it back here!" Sophie crouched down and patted the ground in front of her. Daisy lay down with her mouse.

"Take the mouse back to Sophie, Daisy," Dad scooped up the little collie and her toy and plopped them at Sophie's feet. Daisy looked surprised as Sophie took the mouse toy and threw it across the garden again.

Yip, yip, yip! she barked, racing after it. This time, she ran away when Dad tried to pick her up.

"I'll get the dog biscuits," Sophie said. "They helped when we were training Morris."

Sure enough, when Sophie held out a dog biscuit, Daisy trotted towards her, proudly holding her mouse.

Thpth! Daisy spat out the mouse and took the biscuit.

"Good girl, Daisy!" Sophie and Dad said together. Sophie threw the squeaky toy again.

Daisy's ears pricked up. She ignored the mouse and dashed to the door of the house. A car drew into the drive.

"Mum's back!" Sophie, Dad and Daisy raced through the house and reached the front door just as Mum was opening it. Morris limped in.

Ooof! Morris woofed, sitting down and holding out his poorly paw. It was beautifully bandaged up in a green waterproof dressing.

"Morris!" Sophie squealed, throwing her arms around his neck. "How's his paw?" she asked Mum.

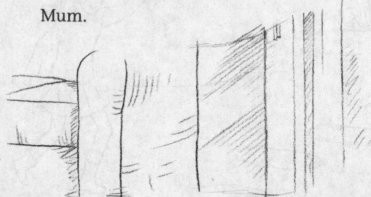

"All cleaned up, but bruised and scraped," Mum said. "We have to be careful for a few days and not let Morris walk on it too much. He was very good at the vet's. He didn't even bark at the cats in the waiting room!"

"Morris, I'm proud of you!" Sophie beamed, giving him a big hug.

Morris's tail thumped on the floor as he looked over Sophie's shoulder. Sophie turned to look too. Daisy was sitting on the mat in front of the fireplace.

Morris's grey muzzle wrinkled as if he was smiling. He limped towards Daisy and gave her a big sloppy lick.

Sluuuurp!

Sophie clapped her hands in delight. "He's saying thank you!" she laughed.

Morris slumped down on the mat beside Daisy. The little collie snuggled up to him. In no time at all, Morris was fast asleep.

Daisy looked up at Sophie. Her white-tipped tail was wagging and her eyes were shining with delight.

"Good girl, Daisy!" Sophie whispered. "You and Morris are going to be the best of friends! From now on, everything will be just perfect!"

Read on for lots more . . .

🐾 🐾 🐾 🐾

Battersea Dogs & Cats Home

Battersea Dogs & Cats Home is a charity that aims never to turn away a dog or cat in need of our help. We reunite lost dogs and cats with their owners; when we can't do this, we care for them until new homes can be found for them; and we educate the public about responsible pet ownership. Every year the Home takes in around 12,000 dogs and cats. In addition to the site in south-west London, the Home also has two other centres based at Old Windsor, Berkshire, and Brands Hatch, Kent.

The original site in Holloway

History

The Temporary Home for Lost and
Starving Dogs was originally opened in a
stable yard in Holloway in 1860 by Mary
Tealby after she found a starving puppy
in the street. There was no one to look
after him, so she took him home and
nursed him back to health. She was so
worried about the other dogs wandering
the streets that she opened the Temporary
Home for Lost and Starving Dogs. The
Home was established to help to look
after them all and find them new homes.

Sadly Mary Tealby died in 1865, aged
sixty-four, and little more is known about
her, but her good work was continued. In
1871 the Home moved to its present site
in Battersea, and was renamed the Dogs'
Home Battersea.

Some important dates for the Home:

1883 – Battersea start taking in cats.

1914 – 100 sledge dogs are housed at the Hackbridge site, in preparation for Ernest Shackleton's second Antarctic expedition.

1956 – Queen Elizabeth II becomes patron of the Home.

2004 – Red the Lurcher's night-time antics become world famous when he is caught on camera regularly escaping from his kennel and liberating his canine chums for midnight feasts.

2007 – The BBC broadcast *Animal Rescue Live* from the Home for three weeks from mid-July to early August.

Amy Watson

Amy Watson has been working at
Battersea Dogs & Cats Home for six years
and has been the Home's Education
Officer for two and a half years. Amy's
role means that she organizes all the
school visits to the Home for children
aged sixteen and under, and regularly
visits schools around Battersea's three

sites to teach children how to behave and
stay safe around dogs and cats, and all
about responsible dog and cat ownership.
She also regularly features on the
Battersea website – www.battersea.org.uk
– giving tips and advice on how to train
your dog or cat under the "Amy's
Answers" section.

On most school visits Amy can take a
dog with her, so she is normally
accompanied by her beautiful ex-
Battersea dog Hattie. Hattie has been
living with Amy for just over a year and
really enjoys meeting new children and
helping Amy with her work.

The process for re-homing a dog or a cat

When a lost dog or cat arrives, Battersea's Lost Dogs & Cats Line works hard to try to find the animal's owners. If, after seven days, they have not been able to reunite them, the search for a new home can begin.

The Home works hard to find caring, permanent new homes for all the lost and unwanted dogs and cats.

Dogs and cats have their own characters and so staff at the Home will spend time getting to know every dog and cat. This helps decide the type of home the dog or cat needs.

There are five stages of the re-homing process at Battersea Dogs & Cats Home. Battersea's re-homing team wants to find you the perfect pet, sometimes this can take a while, so please be patient while we search for your new friend!

1 Application

2 Interview

3 Home visit

4 Searching for a pet

5 Leaving with your new pet

Have a look at our website:
http://www.battersea.org.uk/dogs/ rehoming/index.html for more details!

"Did you know?" questions about dogs and cats

- Puppies do not open their eyes until they are about two weeks old.

- According to *The Guinness Book of Records*, the smallest living dog is a long-haired Chihuahua called Danka Kordak from Slovakia, who is 13.8cm tall and 18.8cm long.

- Dalmatians, with all those cute black spots, are actually born white.

- The greyhound is the fastest dog on earth. They can reach speeds of up to 45 miles per hour.

- The first living creature sent into space was a female dog named Laika.

- Cats spend 15% of their day grooming themselves and a massive 70% of their day sleeping.

- Cats see six times better in the dark than we do.

- A cat's tail helps it to balance when it is on the move – especially when it is jumping.

- The cat, giraffe and camel are the only animals that walk by moving both their left feet, then both their right feet, when walking.

Dos and Don'ts of looking after dogs and cats

Dogs dos and don'ts

DO

- Be gentle and quiet around dogs at all times – treat them how you would like to be treated.
- Have respect for dogs.

DON'T

- Sneak up on a dog – you could scare them.
- Tease a dog – it's not fair.
- Stare at a dog – dogs can find this scary.
- Disturb a dog who is sleeping or eating.

- Assume a dog wants to play with you. Just like you, sometimes they may want to be left alone.
- Approach a dog who is without an owner as you won't know if the dog is friendly or not.

Cats dos and don'ts

DO
- Be gentle and quiet around cats at all times.
- Have respect for cats.
- Let a cat approach you in their own time.

DON'T
- Never stare at a cat as they can find this intimidating.

- Tease a cat – it's not fair.
- Disturb a sleeping or eating cat – they may not want attention or to play.
- Assume a cat will always want to play. Like you, sometimes they want to be left alone.

Here is a delicious recipe for you to follow.

Remember to ask an adult to help you.

Cheddar Cheese Dog Cookies

You will need:

227g grated Cheddar cheese

(use at room temperature)

114g margarine

1 egg

1 clove of garlic (crushed)

172g wholewheat flour

30g wheatgerm

1 teaspoon salt

30ml milk

Preheat the oven to 375°F/190°C/gas mark 5.

Cream the cheese and margarine together.

When smooth, add the egg and garlic and

mix well. Add the flour, wheatgerm and salt. Mix well until a dough forms. Add the milk and mix again.

Chill the mixture in the fridge for one hour.

Roll the dough onto a floured surface until it is about 4cm thick. Use cookie cutters to cut out shapes.

Bake on an ungreased baking tray for 15–18 minutes.

Cool to room temperature and store in an airtight container in the fridge.

Some fun pet-themed puzzles!

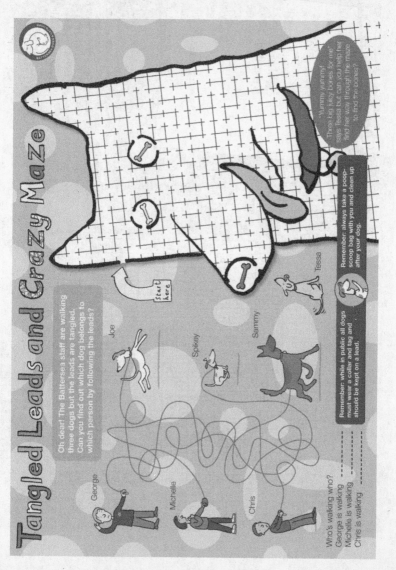

What to think about before getting a dog!

Here is a list of things that you need to think about before getting a dog. See if you can find them in the word search and while you look, think why they might be so important. Only look for words written in blue. They can be written backwards, diagonally, forwards, up and down so look carefully and GOOD LUCK!

SIZE
MALE OR FEMALE
AGE
COST
BEHAVIOUR
BASIC TRAINING
HOUSE TRAINING
TIME ALONE
GOOD WITH: PETS, CHILDREN,
STRANGERS, DOGS
HOW: ENERGETIC, CUDDLY,
INDEPENDENT,
STRONG WILLED, INDEPENDENT,

Can you think of any other things? Write them in the spaces below.

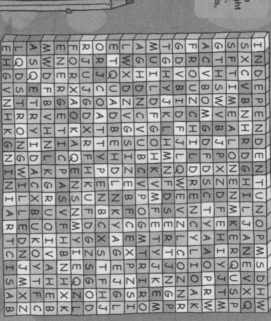

Dog Breeds Crossword

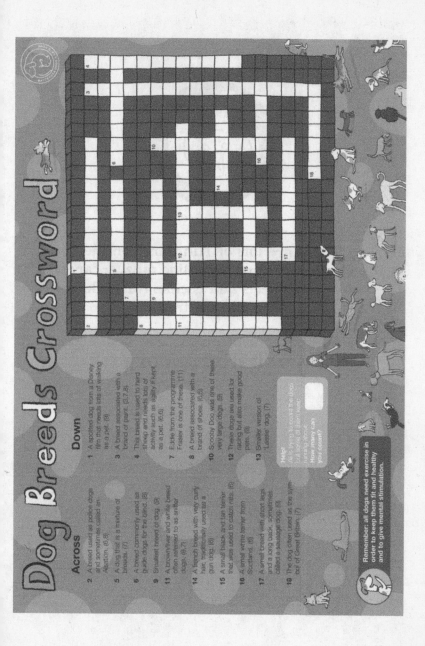

Across

2 A breed used as police dogs and sometimes called an Alsatian. (6,8)

5 A dog that is a mixture of breeds. (7)

6 A breed commonly used as guide dogs for the blind. (8)

9 Smallest breed of dog. (9)

11 A town/river and white breed often referred to as a/after dogs. (8,7)

14 A french breed with very curly hair, traditionally used as a gun dog. (6)

15 A small black and tan terrier that was used to catch rats. (6)

16 A small white terrier from Scotland. (6)

17 A small breed with short legs and a long back, sometimes called a sausage dog. (8)

18 The dog often used as the symbol of Great Britain. (7)

Down

1 A spotted dog from a Disney film that needs lots of walking as a pet. (9)

3 A breed associated with a brand of paint. (3,8)

4 This breed is used to herd sheep and needs lots of activity such as agility if kept as a pet. (6,6)

7 Eddie from the programme Frasier is one of these. (11)

8 A breed associated with a brand of shoes. (6,6)

10 Scooby Doo was one of these very large dogs. (5)

12 These dogs are used for racing but also make good pets. (8)

13 Smaller version of "Lassie" dog. (7)

Help!
Ali is trying to count the dogs but some of them keep running about.
How many can you count?

Remember: all dogs need exercise in order to keep them fit and healthy and to give mental stimulation.

There are lots of fun things on the
website, including an online quiz, e-cards,
colouring sheets and recipes for making
dog and cat treats.

www.battersea.org.uk